"Wheeeeeeee!" said Drum as she rushed around Todd's garden. "Wheeeeeeee!"

Drum was so happy that all she could do was rush around shouting, "Wheeeeeeee!"

Zak, Panzee and Tang tried to calm her down but Drum was just too excited! She was going to stay up late!

3

But the ZingZillas had a problem. Drum could only stay up late if she had a nap in the afternoon. If she didn't have a nap she'd fall asleep during The Big Night Zing.

That would be a disaster!

Somebody had to tell Drum to have a nap.

Drum stopped rushing around for a moment and flopped down on the ground.

Zak gently said. "If you don't have a nap you won't be able to play in The Big Night Zing."

4

5

But when she heard the words
'Big Night Zing',
Drum got really excited again!
"Wheeeeeeee!" she shouted.

She rushed round the garden
again before disappearing
into the jungle.
"Oh dear," said Zak. "I don't
think I should have said that."

Tang knew just the person who could help him get Drum to have a nap and decided to go down to the Coconut Hut.

"I'd better hurry," said Tang. "There's the first coconut!"

But down at the Coconut Hut, Tang didn't find DJ Loose. He found Drum instead, looking a little sleepy.

Tang tried to get Drum to nap. "If you don't have a nap, you'll be too tired to play The Big Night Zing," he said.

As soon as she heard the words **"Big Night Zing"** Drum rushed off again, shouting, **"Wheeeeeeee!"**

Just then, DJ Loose appeared.
"What's the problem, Tang?" he asked.

"I need to get Drum to sleep before The Big Night Zing," sighed
Tang. "But it's difficult because she gets really excited and starts
running around shouting, "Wheeeeeeee!"

DJ had a little think. "Hmm," he said. "Perhaps you need an instrument that plays gentle music. Gentle music might send Drum to sleep."

"That's a brilliant idea!" said Tang. "But what sort of instrument plays gentle music like that?"

"Let's go to the Glade and find out," smiled DJ Loose.

When Tang and DJ Loose got to the Glade, they saw a very big instrument with lots and lots of strings.

It was playing the gentlest music Tang had ever heard!

"What is that instrument, DJ?" Tang asked.

"That is a harp," replied DJ. "You play it by plucking the strings with your fingers. Listen!"

They listened to the harp music. Tang thought it sounded really slow and dreamy. The perfect music to help Drum fall asleep.

Tang was thrilled. "We can play Drum a gentle song to send her to sleep! Thanks, DJ!" He rushed off to find the others.

"Wheeeeeeee!"

13

Gravel and Granite watched
Tang rush past.
"What's happening tonight?"
asked Gravel.

"The ZingZillas are playing a Big
Night Zing," replied Granite. "And
look, there's coconut number two."

"**Wheeeeeeee!**" shouted Gravel.
He was really excited too.

Tang found Zak and Panzee and told them his idea.

"Oh, yes!" said Panzee. "We could play Drum a lullaby. That's a song that helps you fall asleep. But what could we sing about?"

The ZingZillas had a think. Then, Zak had a good idea. "The words could be about the sounds of the Island! The leaves rustling, the seagulls calling and the swooshy sound of the sea!"

Panzee and Tang thought this was a great idea!

Back at the Clubhouse, the ZingZillas played their new song. The beautiful and dreamy music floated through the jungle and Drum heard it. She enjoyed it so much, she crept into Todd's garden and settled down to listen.

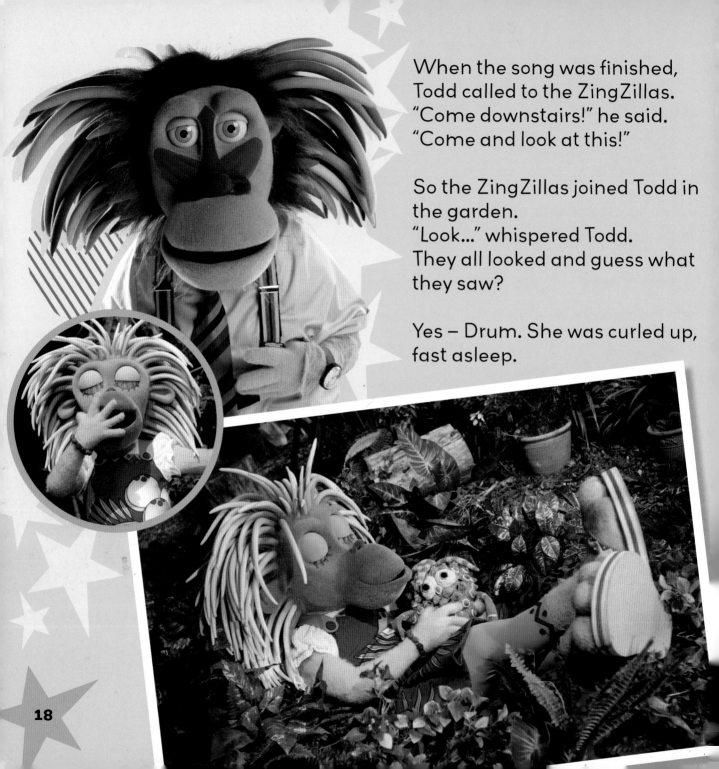

When the song was finished, Todd called to the ZingZillas. "Come downstairs!" he said. "Come and look at this!"

So the ZingZillas joined Todd in the garden.
"Look..." whispered Todd.
They all looked and guess what they saw?

Yes – Drum. She was curled up, fast asleep.

18

"Great," whispered Zak. "Finally she's having a good nap before The Big Night Zing."

But as soon as he said, **'Big Night Zing'**, he wished he hadn't. Drum heard and she jumped up shouting **"Wheeeeeeee!"** before dashing off into the jungle.

"Here we go again," sighed Panzee.

19

It was getting near the Big Night Zing time. The Coconut Clock counted down coconut number three, and Gravel and Granite were getting worried.

The ZingZillas decided to set off into the jungle to find Drum. "Drum! Drum! Where are you?" they called.

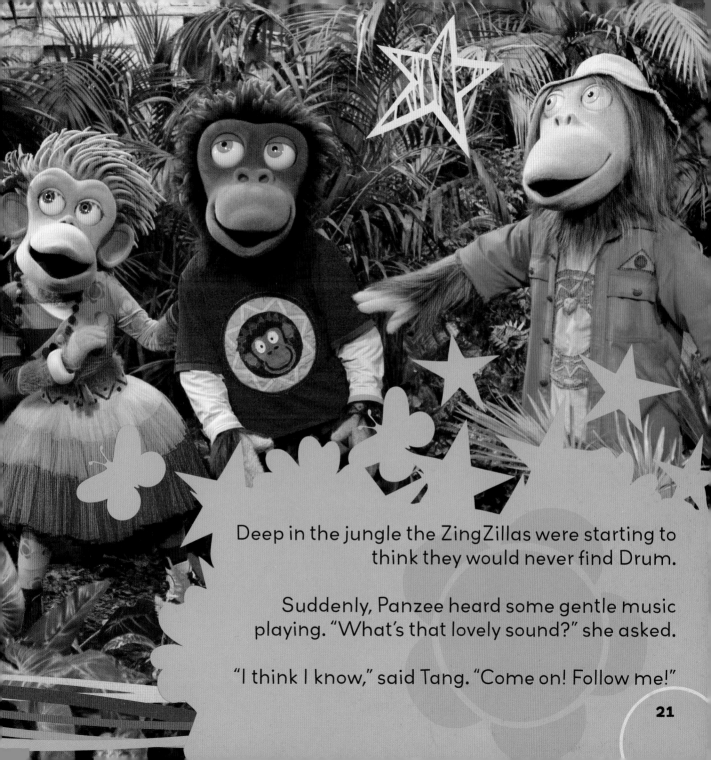

Deep in the jungle the ZingZillas were starting to think they would never find Drum.

Suddenly, Panzee heard some gentle music playing. "What's that lovely sound?" she asked.

"I think I know," said Tang. "Come on! Follow me!"

Tang led Zak and Panzee to the Glade. There was the harp, still playing beautiful music. Curled up nearby and fast asleep, was Drum!

"At last," said Zak. "She's having her nap!"

Panzee saw that the sun was setting. "It's almost time for The Big Zing!" she said.

So, the ZingZillas now had to wake up a very sleepy Drum. "Come on Drum! We've got a song to play!" they laughed.

The last coconut fell as they all dashed down to the beach.

23

And so, when the last coconut had fallen and the Moaning Stones had whizzed round the island, DJ Loose said, "It's that time of the day when we like to say: It's Big Night Zing Time! So take it away!"

And the ZingZillas played a beautiful, gentle **Big Night Zing.** Afterwards, everyone agreed:

That was the best Big Zing EVER.